The Cheeky
Monkey

First published in 2000 by
Franklin Watts
96 Leonard Street
London
EC2A 4XD

Franklin Watts Australia
14 Mars Road
Lane Cove
NSW 2066

A CIP catalogue record for this book is available
from the British Library.

ISBN 0 7496 3710 2

Series Editor: Louise John
Series Advisor: Dr Barrie Wade
Series Designer: Jason Anscomb

Printed in Hong Kong

The Cheeky
Monkey

by Anne Cassidy

Illustrated by Lisa Smith

W
FRANKLIN WATTS
NEW YORK • LONDON • SYDNEY

Wendy woke up late
one day.

She walked into the
garden and found ...

... a monkey sitting in
her treehouse.

"Monkey, get out of my
treehouse!" Wendy shouted.

"No, I'm staying here!"
the monkey shouted back.

Wendy turned purple
with anger.

"Oh no, you're not!"
she shouted.

Wendy made a plan.

She went into battle with
the monkey.

But the monkey had custard pies.

14

"Take that!" he shouted
as he threw them at Wendy.

Wendy needed a new plan.

She went to have a look

in her toy box.

Wendy became a pirate.

She was going to capture
the treehouse.

The monkey became a
pirate, too.

He shot at Wendy with
hundreds of peanuts.

So Wendy became
a cowgirl.

She made a plan to capture the monkey.

But the monkey had a
better plan and Wendy
got very wet.

The monkey laughed and laughed.

Wendy made another plan.

She went into the kitchen.

Wendy made a trap for the monkey.

He came straight down
from the treehouse ...

... and got straight into Wendy's bed!

Leapfrog has been specially designed to fit the requirements of the National Literacy Strategy. It offers real books for beginning readers by top authors and illustrators.

There are five other humorous stories to choose from:

The Bossy Cockerel   ISBN 0 7946 3708 0

Written by **Margaret Nash**, illustrated by **Elisabeth Moseng**

A traditional farmyard story with a twist. Charlie the Cockerel is very bossy indeed.
The hens think it's time he got his come-uppance ...

Bill's Baggy Trousers   ISBN 0 7496 3709 9

Written by **Susan Gates**, illustrated by **Anni Axworthy**

A frivolous fantasy story about Bill and his new, baggy trousers, which turn out to be a lot more fun than he could have imagined!

Mr Spotty's Potty   ISBN 0 7496 3711 0

Written by **Hilary Robinson**, illustrated by **Peter Utton**

A rhyming text with repetitive and patterned language about Mr Spotty's attempts to grow seeds in an old potty. It soon becomes clear that Dot, his dog, may be the reason behind his success.

Little Joe's Big Race   ISBN 0 7496 3712 9

Written by **Andy Blackford**, illustrated by **Tim Archbold**

An outrageously silly story about the adventures of Little Joe as he runs an egg and spoon race that turns out to be more of an experience than he bargained for!

The Little Star   ISBN 0 7496 3713 7

Written by **Deborah Nash**, illustrated by **Richard Morgan**

A fantasy story with an element of humour about a little star who no longer wants to live in the sky. His friend, the Moon, takes him on a magical journey to show him how much fun the sky can be.